KING OF ICE

The Price of Power

Presii

The characters and events portrayed in this book are fictitious. Any similarity to real persons, living or dead, is coincidental and not intended by the author.

ISBN-13: 979-8-218-51388-7

Cover design by: Muhammad Sabir Shah
Printed in the United States of America

"Every king sits on a throne of sacrifice, built by those who fell before him."

PRESII

PREFACE

As someone who's faced struggles and found success, I've learned that power always comes with a cost. "King of Ice" is a story that reflects not only ambition and survival, but also the choices we make when everything is on the line.

Jaylin "Ice" Carter, the main character, rises from the bottom to control the streets of Westbrook, but his journey is far from easy. It's filled with decisions that come at a price–whether it's trust, loyalty, or personal sacrifices. Ice's story speaks to the hustle, the grind, and the constant pressure of holding onto power in a world where it can vanish in an instant.

While this book explores a fictional world, it's inspired by the realities many people face in their pursuit of something bigger. It's about ambition, yes, but also about what it takes to stay on top once you've gotten there. The world Ice moves through is one where respect is earned with blood, and keeping it requires making the hardest choices.

"King of Ice" is a tale of survival, ambition, and the high price of power. For some, the climb to the top is worth it, but as Ice's story shows, every throne comes with its own set of challenges–and consequences. – Presii

CHAPTER 1: A HUSTLER'S RISE

Jaylin "Ice" Carter wasn't born into power. He took it—piece by bloody piece. The streets of Westbrook were as unforgiving as they were full of opportunity. By the time Ice hit his mid-20s, he had become the go-to plug for the best weed in the city. It wasn't the hardest hustle, but it kept money in his pockets and respect on his name. In Westbrook, respect could vanish just as quickly as it was earned. Tonight, Ice was about to learn just how dangerous this truth was.

The streetlights flickered over Ice's black BMW as he cruised through the city. Westbrook was alive at night—its pulse visible in neon reflections off the wet pavement and in the hurried steps of people chasing highs and money. But Ice wasn't distracted. His mind was locked on one thing: Maceo. A local dealer, Maceo had been shorting Ice on their latest deals, and that kind of mistake could turn deadly.

Ice parked outside **The Spot**, a dimly lit club where business blurred with pleasure. The pounding bass reverberated through the walls, and smoke hung in the air like a thick fog. Ice scanned the crowd for Maceo. Spotting him in the VIP section, lounging as if he didn't owe Ice money, sent a jolt of anger through him.

Dre, Ice's right-hand man, trailed closely behind as they cut through the crowd. As they passed, women's hands reached out, brushing against Ice, drawn to him like moths to a flame. But tonight wasn't about pleasure—it was all business.

"Yo, Ice!" one of the girls called, her voice slurred as she tried to grab his arm.

"Not tonight," Ice muttered, brushing her off without breaking his stride.

They approached the VIP booth where Maceo sat with two girls on either side of him, a bottle of liquor on the table in front of them. Maceo flashed a wide grin, but it quickly faded when Ice sat across from him, cold and silent.

"You know why I'm here," Ice said, his voice low and dangerous.

Maceo stammered, his confidence slipping. "I-I got the money, Ice. I just need a little more time."

Before Maceo could finish, Dre grabbed him by the collar, yanking him out of his seat and slamming him against the back of the booth. "You think this is a joke?" Dre snarled.

Ice didn't flinch. "You short me again, and you won't get to ask for more time."

Maceo's eyes widened with fear as he nodded frantically. "It won't happen again, I swear."

Ice stared him down for a moment, then leaned back in his seat. "Make sure it doesn't." He stood up, adjusting his jacket. Without another word, he and Dre left, leaving Maceo shaken and the girls frozen in stunned silence.

CHAPTER 2: PLEASURE AND POWER

Later that night, Ice stood by the floor-to-ceiling window in his penthouse, gazing out at the glittering skyline of Westbrook. The city below thrummed with life, but his mind was far from at ease. Maceo had been dealt with, but Ice knew that selling weed wasn't going to take him to the top. If he wanted to control the streets, he needed something bigger.

Tasha, the one woman who had been with him through it all, walked up behind him. She slid her arms around his waist, pressing her body against his back. Tasha had seen Ice at his lowest, long before the money started rolling in. She understood the weight of what he carried, but tonight she could feel the tension in him.

"You're pushing too hard," she said softly, her breath warm against his neck.

Ice didn't turn around. His gaze stayed fixed on the city lights. "I've barely started, Tasha. There's more to come."

Tasha tightened her hold on him, pulling him closer. "Every time you leave, I wonder if you'll make it back."

Ice turned to face her, finally breaking his focus on the city outside. Tasha's dark eyes looked up at him, filled with both love and concern. He kissed her softly, his hands moving down to her hips, pulling her against him. "You don't need to worry about me," he whispered against her lips. "I've got it all under control."

Tasha's hands roamed his chest, her touch soft but filled with desire. The tension between them thickened as Ice leaned down, kissing her deeply. Without breaking the kiss, he picked her up, her legs wrapping around his waist as he carried her toward the bedroom. Their clothes fell to the floor, piece by piece, until they were skin to skin, and Ice could feel the heat between them.

By the time they reached the bed, Tasha was fully exposed, her body a perfect reflection of the fire burning inside her. Ice kissed her neck, his lips trailing down her chest, making her moan softly as he explored every inch of her skin. Tasha arched her back, her body trembling with anticipation as Ice's mouth moved lower, teasing her with his tongue.

"Jay," she gasped, her voice thick with need.

Ice took his time, savoring every moment. Her moans grew louder, her fingers gripping the sheets as he pushed her closer and closer to the edge. Her body quivered as waves of pleasure coursed through her, and just when she thought she couldn't take it anymore, Ice pushed her over the edge. Her climax hit her hard, her cries filling the room as she shuddered beneath him.

But Ice wasn't done.

He climbed on top of her, his body pressing against hers as he entered her slowly, deeply. Tasha's eyes glazed over with pleasure as she wrapped her legs around him, pulling him closer. Their bodies moved together in perfect rhythm, the tension between them rising with every thrust.

“I want you,” she whispered breathlessly, her nails digging into his back.

Ice’s movements quickened, the intensity between them growing until they were both on the edge of release. The bed creaked beneath them, the sounds of their passion filling the room as they reached their climax together, their bodies trembling in unison.

As they lay there afterward, Tasha rested her head on Ice’s chest, her fingers tracing lazy circles on his skin. But even as the warmth of their intimacy lingered, Ice’s mind was already racing. The streets were always waiting, and the higher you climbed, the more dangerous the fall.

CHAPTER 3: A DANGEROUS PROPOSITION

The next morning, Ice sat in the living room of his penthouse, surrounded by stacks of cash. The weed game had been good to him, but the money wasn't coming in fast enough. He knew if he wanted to control Westbrook, he needed to level up. The problem was, the higher the stakes, the greater the risk. Ice wasn't afraid of the risk, but he needed a way in.

The sound of the elevator ding echoed through the apartment as Darnell walked in, carrying the weight of experience with him. Darnell was older, wiser, and had been deep in the game long before Ice had made a name for himself. He had connections and knowledge that could shift Ice's position in the streets.

Darnell sat down on the couch across from Ice, lighting a cigarette. "You ever think about cooking?" he asked casually, blowing smoke as if the question was no big deal.

Ice raised an eyebrow, intrigued. "Cooking?"

"Not the petty weed you've been moving," Darnell said with a smirk. "I'm talking about crack. The money's faster, and the streets are hungry for it. You learn how to cook, and you'll have Westbrook in your pocket."

Ice leaned forward, resting his elbows on his knees. Crack was a whole different game. The money was better, the demand higher, but the risk? It was lethal. Still, Ice had been waiting for a way to break through to the next level, and this sounded like his chance.

"You show me how," Ice said, his voice steady. "And I'll take over this city."

Darnell gave him a long, considering look. "You sure you're ready for that? Once you're in, there's no turning back."

Ice didn't hesitate. "I'm ready."

Darnell nodded, flicking ash into the tray. "Alright, I'll teach you. But understand, you'll be stepping into a whole different world. The game changes when you start pushing weight like this. People start watching you differently. The cops, other dealers... You slip up once, and that's it."

"I don't make mistakes," Ice replied, his tone cold and determined.

Darnell smiled slightly. "We'll see about that. Meet me tonight, and I'll show you how it's done."

Ice leaned back, a sense of excitement building inside him. This was the move he had been waiting for. Learning how to cook crack meant stepping into a league most people were afraid to enter. But for Ice, it was just another step toward domination.

That evening, Ice pulled up to a rundown apartment building on the edge of town. The place looked abandoned, with broken windows and trash littering the sidewalk. But this was where Darnell did his work. Ice wasn't fazed. He knew real business didn't happen in flashy penthouses or fancy clubs—it happened in places no one cared to look.

Ice walked up the creaky stairs, the dim hallway reeking of cigarettes and old beer. He knocked twice on the door at the end of the hall, and Darnell opened it, waving him in.

Inside, the apartment was bare except for a few old chairs and a stained mattress in the corner. But on the kitchen counter sat the tools of the trade: a digital scale, a 8 ounce glass Pyrex, and a box of baking soda. The room fell quiet, Ice focused, and Darnell just watching, ready to guide him through every step.

"You ready for this?" Darnell asked, leaning back against the counter.

Ice nodded. "Let's do it."

Darnell pulled out a tightly sealed bag of cocaine and tossed it to Ice. "Thirty-one grams," he said. "This ain't the little shit you've been dealing with. This is how you make real money."

Ice felt the weight of the bag in his hand. He knew this was about to change everything. He tore the bag open, pouring the cocaine into the Pyrex.

CHAPTER 4: LEARNING TO COOK

Darnell didn't waste any time. The apartment was dimly lit, its peeling walls and broken windows casting an eerie feel. But for Ice, this was just business. His focus was locked on the tools laid out on the counter: a digital scale, a 8 ounce glass Pyrex, and a box of baking soda. Tonight was the night everything changed.

"You ready for this?" Darnell asked, his voice calm but sharp.

Ice nodded, feeling the weight of the cocaine in his hands– 31 grams, far beyond the small-time weed deals he'd been used to. This was a different game, and he knew it.

Darnell gestured to the Pyrex. "Start by breaking that down."

Ice tore the bag open and poured the 31 grams of cocaine into the Pyrex. The block was solid, slightly crystallized. Ice grabbed a fork and began working the coke, breaking it into a fine powder with precise motions.

"Good. Now fill it halfway with water," Darnell instructed.

Ice did as he was told, filling the Pyrex halfway with water, watching as the powder dissolved into the liquid.

"Next, grab that box of baking soda," Darnell said. "Measure out exactly three grams."

Ice carefully scooped out three grams of baking soda and measured it on the digital scale. He poured the baking soda into the Pyrex, watching as the mixture began to bubble slightly.

"This is the part that separates the cocaine oil from the water," Darnell explained. "When you melt it down, you'll see the oil. If not, it'll just look clear."

Ice nodded, fully focused on each step.

"Now, put it in the microwave," Darnell continued. "But listen closely—never on high heat. You just want it to melt down slowly. Keep checking it, but don't overcook it."

Ice placed the Pyrex in the microwave, set the heat to low, and stood there watching. He opened the microwave every so often, making sure the mixture wasn't overheating. Slowly, it began to melt, the powder dissolving into the water.

After a few minutes, Darnell nodded. "Now comes the tricky part. Take it out and bring it over to the sink. I already set up a pot in there."

Ice carefully removed the Pyrex and walked it over to the sink, where a large pot was in place.

"You want to sprinkle cold water into the hot mixture," Darnell instructed, pointing to the Pyrex. "This'll make the cocaine oil separate from the water and drop to the bottom."

Ice followed Darnell's instructions, gently sprinkling cold water into the Pyrex. As soon as the cold water hit, the cocaine oil dropped to the bottom, separating from the water like liquid gold.

Darnell gave a nod of approval. “That’s why you use the pot. If the Pyrex gets too hot and cracks, you don’t want to lose your work down the drain.”

Ice carefully poured off the excess water, leaving about a quarter inch of water floating over the golden oil sitting at the bottom of the Pyrex.

“Don’t leave too much water,” Darnell said. “That’s important for the next step.”

Ice placed the Pyrex flat on the counter. Darnell handed him the scale again. “Now, measure out exactly five grams of baking soda.”

Ice measured five grams and poured it into the Pyrex. Darnell’s tone became more urgent. “Now you’ve got to move fast. Whip it.”

Ice grabbed the fork and began whipping the mixture in quick, circular motions, his wrist moving with precision.

“Whip it like you’re beating eggs,” Darnell instructed, his eyes focused on the Pyrex. “If you don’t mix it well enough, the coke, water, and baking soda won’t lock together when it hardens. But if you whip it too long, it’ll harden while you’re still stirring.”

Ice whipped the mixture faster, his focus locked in. The consistency began to change, turning creamy and milky.

“All right, stop!” Darnell commanded suddenly.

Ice immediately stopped and set the Pyrex flat on the counter, watching as the mixture started to solidify.

"That's it," Darnell said, satisfied. "Now let it sit."

Seconds passed, and Ice watched as the creamy mixture hardened into a solid mass at the bottom of the Pyrex.

"Now take this," Darnell said, handing him a razor blade, "and work it around the edges carefully. You don't want to break the product."

Ice carefully worked the blade around the edges of the now-hardened mass, slowly loosening it from the Pyrex. Finally, with a gentle push, the crack popped out in one solid piece.

"That's dope boy magic," Darnell said with a grin.

Ice placed the solid piece of crack on the digital scale. It weighed 45.3 grams.

Ice couldn't believe it. "Forty-five," he muttered, staring at the numbers on the scale.

Darnell nodded. "That's how you flip it. But listen—if you ever mess up, don't panic. You can always start the process over. You can recook it more than once."

Ice nodded, taking it all in.

Darnell handed him a sandwich bag. "Bag it up."

Ice placed the crack into the sandwich bag, tying it tightly. Darnell handed him two more bags. "Double-bag it, then triple-bag it."

Ice did as he was told, triple-bagging the crack tightly.

"You're not doing this to keep it fresh," Darnell said, his voice serious. "You're doing it to keep it from losing water weight. When you're ready to sell it, you want it to be as close to that original weight as possible."

Ice placed the triple-bagged crack in the freezer as instructed, feeling the rush of accomplishment. This was how real money was made.

“Leave it there overnight,” Darnell continued. “It won’t lose any more water weight by the time you’re ready to sell it.”

Ice closed the freezer, the weight of what he’d just learned hitting him hard. He had just unlocked a new level in the game.

Darnell clapped him on the back. “You did good, Ice. Real good. Now, you’re ready to take over.”

CHAPTER 5: THE NEW HUSTLE

By the time Ice had mastered the cooking process, the game had changed for him. Crack wasn't like weed—it moved faster, the demand was higher, and the money came quicker than Ice could count. With his new skill and Darnell's backing, Ice was no longer just another street dealer. He was on his way to becoming a kingpin, and everyone on the streets of Westbrook knew it.

The money was rolling in. Ice's phone buzzed nonstop with new orders, and his crew expanded to meet the rising demand. Every night, the stacks of cash on Ice's table grew taller. His name was being whispered in every corner of the city.

But as his operation grew, so did the pressure.

One evening, Ice and Dre sat in Ice's penthouse, overlooking the glowing city below. Stacks of cash were piled on the coffee table between them. Dre, ever loyal, lit a blunt and exhaled smoke, his gaze fixed on the horizon.

"We're moving faster than anyone in the game," Dre said, his voice low. "But word is, Rico's not happy about it."

Rico was a name that carried weight in Westbrook. He had

been running the crack game for years, but now, with Ice's quick rise, his grip on the streets was loosening.

Ice nodded, counting the money in front of him, calm and composed. "Let him be mad. He's losing ground because we're stretching the product better than anyone."

Ice had mastered how to stretch the crack from 31 grams to something more, maximizing profits with every flip. This gave him an edge over other dealers who stuck to the basics. He wasn't just playing the game—he was rewriting the rules.

Dre took a drag from the blunt, blowing smoke toward the ceiling. "Rico's been in this game too long to just sit back and let us take over. Word is, he's planning to make a move."

Ice knew Dre was right. The streets were buzzing with rumors about Rico's next move. The game wasn't just about making money anymore—it was about staying alive.

"We'll be ready for him," Ice said, his voice cool. "But we're not backing down."

Dre nodded, but the tension in the room was thick. Ice knew that the streets weren't just watching—they were waiting. Every successful dealer in Westbrook was watching Ice's rise, and with that came enemies. Rico was just the first of many.

"We keep moving," Ice said, leaning back on the couch, his gaze turning toward the window. The city lights sparkled below, but Ice knew it was only a matter of time before the streets came knocking.

The climb to the top had been fast, but staying there would

be the real challenge. And Ice was prepared for whatever came next.

CHAPTER 6: POWER AND PRESSURE

The days moved fast as Ice's operation continued to expand. With every deal, every flip, his pockets grew deeper, and his reputation stretched across the city. But with success came pressure—more eyes on him, more people wanting a piece of what he had built.

Ice stood in his penthouse one evening, watching the city lights flicker beneath him. The noise of Westbrook buzzed below, but in his world, it felt quieter than usual. It was the calm before the storm—he could feel it.

Dre walked in, his expression serious. He had been out all day, gathering information and making sure Ice stayed on top. But the look in Dre's eyes told Ice that something wasn't right.

"We got a problem," Dre said, his voice low but urgent.

Ice didn't turn away from the window. He had known something was coming, but he was always prepared. "What's the word?"

"Rico's crew is making moves. They've been creeping through the blocks, asking about our spots," Dre said, taking a seat on the couch.

Ice's jaw tightened. Rico wasn't just some street-level dealer. He was smart, ruthless, and had been running Westbrook's game long before Ice came into the picture. But Ice knew Rico was feeling the pressure of losing territory, losing customers. And when a man like Rico was cornered, he became dangerous.

"They tryna push up on us?" Ice asked, still calm.

Dre nodded. "That's the word in the streets. They think we're vulnerable, and they're trying to hit us where it hurts —our supply line."

Ice finally turned, his eyes cold. "We're not letting that happen."

Dre nodded in agreement. "I've already got people watching the spots. Ain't nobody getting close without us knowing."

Ice sat down, his mind running through the possibilities. Rico's move was predictable, but that didn't make it any less dangerous. One wrong slip, one missed opportunity, and everything Ice had built could come crashing down. But Ice wasn't about to let that happen.

"What's the plan, Ice?" Dre asked, leaning forward.

Ice paused for a moment, his eyes narrowing in thought. "We're not going to react too fast. That's what Rico expects. He's waiting for us to make the wrong move."

Dre listened closely, knowing that Ice's calm demeanor wasn't a sign of weakness—it was how he stayed in control.

"I'll get word out," Ice continued. "We tighten up on every spot. Rico wants to play games, let him. But when we strike, we do it smart. We're going to take what's his without him even realizing it."

Dre's face broke into a grin. "That's what I'm talking about."

But Ice wasn't smiling. The streets were watching, waiting for a slip-up, and he couldn't afford one. Rico's crew had been around for too long to just roll over, and Ice knew the next few weeks would be critical. He wasn't just fighting to stay on top—he was fighting for survival.

As Dre left to handle business, Ice poured himself a drink and sat back, his mind still running. The game was no longer just about money. Power came with a price, and the more Ice gained, the more people wanted to take it from him.

The phone on the table buzzed, interrupting his thoughts. It was Tasha.

"You coming through tonight?" she asked, her voice smooth over the line.

Ice smiled slightly, leaning back in his chair. "Yeah, I'll be there in a bit."

Tasha was one of the few things that kept Ice grounded. In a world full of chaos, she was the one constant he could count on. But even with her, the weight of the streets was always looming over him.

He hung up the phone and downed his drink. The calm that had settled over his empire was starting to shift, and Ice knew that every move from now on would determine whether he stayed on top or fell like so many others before him.

CHAPTER 7: UNDER FIRE

The tension in Westbrook was thick enough to cut with a knife. Weeks had passed since Dre's warning about Rico's crew, and Ice had been playing his cards carefully, tightening his grip on every corner of his empire. Rico hadn't made a direct move yet, but Ice knew it was coming—he could feel it in the streets.

Ice sat in his penthouse, reviewing a new batch of orders that had come in. The hustle was steady, the money was rolling, but the calm before the storm lingered in the back of his mind. He glanced at his phone, expecting updates from Dre or one of his soldiers.

Suddenly, the phone rang. Ice answered, and Dre's voice came through, tense and urgent.

"They're coming for us, Ice. Rico's crew is rolling up on the spot over on Fifth right now."

Ice stood up, his heart rate kicking up a notch, but his expression remained ice-cold. "How many?"

"Four cars, fully loaded," Dre replied, his voice tight. "They're bringing heat. They want to shut us down."

Ice knew this was it—the moment Rico had been waiting

for. The power struggle between them had come to a boiling point, and now it was about to erupt into violence. Ice didn't flinch, though. He had been preparing for this.

"Hold them off," Ice ordered. "I'm on my way."

Ice grabbed his Glock from the table and slid it into his waistband. There was no time to waste. He had been expecting this, and now he was ready to defend what he had built.

Fifth Street was alive with tension as Ice pulled up in his black BMW. The streetlights flickered over the scene, and Ice's crew was already in position, weapons drawn, waiting for the inevitable clash.

Dre ran over to Ice as he stepped out of the car, his face grim. "They're right around the corner. They've got automatic weapons, shotguns—you name it."

Ice nodded, scanning the area. "How many of our guys are in position?"

"Ten," Dre replied. "We've got every angle covered."

Ice looked at Dre, then back at the corner where Rico's crew was preparing to move in. His heart pounded in his chest, but his mind was sharp. This wasn't just about protecting his territory—it was about sending a message.

"We're not backing down," Ice said, his voice low but firm. "When they roll through, light them up. No hesitation."

Dre's face hardened with determination. "I got you."

The air was thick with anticipation as Ice and his crew took their positions, guns at the ready. The distant rumble of engines grew louder, and soon the headlights of Rico's crew's cars pierced through the darkness. They were rolling in hard—four black SUVs, all windows down, weapons glinting in the dim light.

Ice's grip tightened on his Glock. This was it. Everything had led to this moment.

The first SUV screeched around the corner, and without waiting for a word, Dre opened fire, the crack of gunshots echoing through the street. Bullets ripped through the windshield of the lead SUV, shattering glass and sending the vehicle swerving. The driver lost control, slamming into a parked car as gunfire erupted from both sides.

Ice stayed calm, stepping into the chaos with precision. He raised his Glock and fired, hitting one of Rico's soldiers square in the chest as he tried to duck behind a car. The man went down, blood splattering the pavement.

The second SUV stopped short, its doors flying open as more of Rico's men jumped out, spraying bullets in every direction. Ice's crew was ready, though. They fired back, their shots clean and deliberate, picking off the attackers one by one.

Dre ducked behind a car, his shotgun blasting as he took down another one of Rico's men who had tried to flank them. The street was a war zone—bullets flying, bodies dropping, and the sound of tires screeching as Rico's crew tried to maneuver out of the ambush.

Ice moved like a ghost through the battlefield, his eyes sharp and his aim deadly. He fired two more shots, dropping another man who had been firing recklessly from behind an open car door. The roar of gunfire filled the air, but Ice remained cool, methodical.

Suddenly, one of the SUVs came barreling toward Ice, the driver flooring it in a desperate attempt to ram him. Ice didn't flinch. He stepped to the side, raised his Glock, and fired straight into the driver's side window. The bullet hit its mark, and the SUV veered off course, crashing into a fire hydrant with a deafening screech of metal.

Water sprayed into the air as the SUV crumpled to a halt, the driver slumped over the wheel, lifeless.

The gunfire began to die down, the chaos settling as Rico's crew realized they were outmatched. One by one, the remaining men dropped their weapons, some trying to run, others collapsing to the ground, wounded.

Dre walked over to Ice, his face slick with sweat but his eyes gleaming with victory. "They're retreating," he said, his voice breathless. "We hit them hard."

Ice nodded, surveying the scene. The street was littered with broken glass, bullet-riddled cars, and bodies. But his crew stood tall, still in control, still alive.

"Let them run," Ice said, lowering his gun. "This isn't over. But tonight, we showed them who owns these streets."

Dre grinned, wiping his brow. "We made a statement."

Ice holstered his Glock, the adrenaline still coursing through him. The battle had been won, but he knew this war was far from over. Rico wouldn't take this loss lightly. He'd be back, and when he did, Ice would be ready.

As Ice and his crew started to regroup, sirens wailed in the distance. The police were coming, but Ice didn't flinch. They had done what they needed to do, and the message was clear: Westbrook belonged to him now.

CHAPTER 8: AFTERMATH

The sirens grew louder as Ice and his crew began to move out. The street was a mess—shattered glass, crumpled cars, and bloodstains on the pavement. But Ice didn't linger. He knew how things worked in Westbrook. The cops would roll through, ask a few questions, and clean up the bodies. But by then, Ice and his crew would be long gone, leaving no trace behind.

Dre was already coordinating the exit, making sure everyone knew where to go. The rest of Ice's crew began to scatter, disappearing into the shadows before the police even had a chance to arrive.

Ice holstered his Glock, his heartbeat finally beginning to slow down. The fight was over, for now, but the weight of what had just happened pressed heavily on his mind. He had won the battle, but he knew this was just the start of a larger war.

Dre jogged over to him, wiping blood from his brow. "We hit 'em hard, Ice. Rico's gonna feel that one."

Ice nodded, his gaze still sharp. "We sent a message, but Rico ain't the type to back down. He's gonna come harder next time."

Dre grimaced but didn't argue. "You think we'll hear from him soon?"

Ice nodded. "Yeah. But we'll be ready."

The two men stood there for a moment longer, the hum of the city filling the silence between them. Then, Ice turned and headed toward his car. "Get the boys back to base. We need to regroup."

Dre gave a short nod and jogged off, making sure the crew was on the move. Ice slid into the driver's seat of his BMW, the engine rumbling to life beneath him. He didn't waste time. He peeled out of the block and headed back to his penthouse. There was too much on his mind to stay in the streets tonight.

Back at the penthouse, Ice sat alone in the living room, his glass of whiskey untouched on the table in front of him. The adrenaline from the shootout had faded, leaving behind a gnawing feeling of unease. He knew the streets were going to be different after tonight. Rico wasn't going to let this go easily.

Tasha walked in, her eyes scanning Ice's face. She could see the tension in him. "You alright?"

Ice didn't answer right away. He leaned back in his chair, staring at the ceiling for a moment before speaking. "It's getting more dangerous out there."

Tasha moved toward him, her fingers gently brushing his shoulder. "I know. I worry about you every time you leave."

Ice let out a sigh, rubbing his temples. He had come a long way since his days of selling weed on the corner, but the stakes were getting higher with every move he made. Rico wasn't going to stop until one of them was dead, and Ice knew he had to stay ahead of the game.

"Rico came for us tonight," Ice finally said, his voice low. "We handled it, but it's far from over."

Tasha's grip tightened on his shoulder. "Jay, you've got so much now. You've built an empire. But what's the point if you're not around to enjoy it?"

Ice didn't respond. He knew she was right, but he couldn't afford to think that way. The streets demanded focus, strategy, and control. Any sign of weakness could get him killed, and Ice wasn't ready to lose everything he had worked for.

"I'll be fine," Ice said, his voice distant. "I always am."

Tasha didn't press the issue, but she stayed close, her presence grounding him in a way that nothing else could. For a moment, Ice let himself relax, his mind drifting away from the chaos outside.

The next morning, Dre showed up at the penthouse, his face grim. Ice was at the kitchen counter, sipping coffee, already prepared for whatever news Dre was bringing.

"You're not gonna like this," Dre said, dropping a newspaper on the counter. The headline read: *Gang Violence Erupts in Westbrook—Multiple Dead in Shootout.*

Ice's eyes scanned the article quickly. It was vague, but the implications were clear. The cops were on high alert, and the city was buzzing about the battle between Ice and Rico's crews. The streets were heating up, and Ice knew this kind of attention was dangerous.

“They’re looking for answers,” Dre said, his voice low. “And they’re gonna start pressing people.”

Ice set the paper down, his mind racing. “Rico’s gonna try to turn this heat on us.”

Dre nodded. “That’s what I’m thinking.”

Ice stood up, pacing the kitchen. He had built his empire on staying low-key, keeping his operation tight. But now, with the spotlight on them, things were getting complicated. The last thing Ice needed was the cops sniffing around his business.

“We need to tighten up,” Ice said, his voice cold and sharp. “Clean everything. No mistakes, no loose ends.”

Dre nodded, already taking out his phone to start giving orders. “You got it.”

But Ice knew it wouldn’t be that simple. Rico was wounded, but he wasn’t down for good. He’d strike back, and when he did, Ice had to be ready for whatever came next.

CHAPTER 9: A CITY ON EDGE

The city was different now. Word had spread quickly about the shootout, and Westbrook was buzzing with tension. Rico's crew had taken a serious hit, but Ice knew better than to assume it was over. The streets were hot, and everyone was waiting for the next move. The cops were sniffing around, and more eyes were on Ice than ever before.

Inside Ice's penthouse, the atmosphere was thick with tension. Dre, Tasha, and a few of Ice's top lieutenants were gathered in the living room, discussing how to keep things tight in the coming weeks. Ice sat at the head of the table, his mind working through every possibility, every angle. He had to stay sharp, now more than ever.

"Cops have been questioning people up and down Fifth Street," Dre said, his arms crossed over his chest. "They're looking for leads, but so far no one's talking."

"They won't find anything," Ice replied, his voice cold and calm. "We cleaned up, and there's no trail back to us."

One of the lieutenants, a younger guy named Marcus, chimed in. "What about Rico's people? You think he's gonna retaliate?"

Ice glanced at Marcus, his eyes hard. "Rico's smart. He's licking his wounds, but he's not out yet. He'll come back, and when he does, we need to be ready."

Tasha, sitting beside Ice, reached out and placed her hand on his. She could feel the weight he was carrying. The pressure was mounting, but she knew he wouldn't back down.

"Do we go after him first?" Dre asked, his voice low but serious.

Ice leaned back in his chair, considering the idea. "Not yet. We keep playing smart. Let him make the next move. When he does, we'll be ready."

That night, Ice sat alone in his office, the city lights casting a faint glow through the windows. The weight of the streets was pressing down on him harder than ever. He had always thrived under pressure, but this time felt different. The stakes were higher, the risks greater. One wrong move, and everything he had built could crumble.

The phone on his desk buzzed, snapping him out of his thoughts. Ice picked it up, recognizing Dre's number.

"What's up?" Ice asked.

Dre's voice came through tense. "We got a problem."

Ice's body tensed. "What kind of problem?"

"One of Rico's men—someone's talking," Dre said, his voice steady but urgent. "Word is, he's been feeding the cops info, trying to flip on us."

Ice's jaw clenched. A rat in Rico's camp wasn't surprising, but it complicated things. If someone started talking to the cops, it could blow everything wide open.

“Who is it?” Ice asked, his voice cold.

“Guy named Sonny. Rico’s second cousin,” Dre replied. “He’s been laying low, but I’ve got a line on him.”

Ice’s mind was already working. A snitch was the last thing they needed right now, especially with the cops already circling. This had to be handled, and fast.

“Where is he?” Ice asked.

“He’s staying at some motel out on the west side,” Dre answered. “You want me to handle it?”

Ice paused for a moment, considering. This wasn’t just about shutting Sonny up—it was about sending a message. If Rico’s people saw that Ice wasn’t afraid to clean house, it would make them think twice about crossing him again.

“No,” Ice finally said. “I’ll handle it.”

Later that night, Ice and Dre pulled up to the rundown motel on the outskirts of Westbrook. The place was a dump—broken windows, peeling paint, and a flickering neon sign that barely worked. It was the kind of place where people went to disappear.

Ice stepped out of the car, his Glock tucked into the waistband of his jeans. He had no intention of making this a quiet affair. This was about making a statement.

Dre walked beside him as they moved toward the motel room where Sonny was hiding out. Ice could feel the adrenaline pumping through his veins, but his face remained calm, unreadable.

They reached the door. Ice knocked twice, the sound echoing in the otherwise silent night. Moments later, the door creaked open, and Sonny's face appeared, wide-eyed and filled with fear.

"Yo, Ice—man, I was just—"

Ice didn't let him finish. He shoved the door open, forcing Sonny back into the room. Dre followed, shutting the door behind them.

"You were just what?" Ice asked, his voice low but deadly.

Sonny backed up, his hands raised. "Look, man, I wasn't gonna say anything to the cops, I swear! They just—they just grabbed me up, man. I didn't have a choice."

Ice stepped closer, his eyes locking onto Sonny's. "You always have a choice."

Sonny swallowed hard, his back pressed against the dingy wall. "Please, Ice. I ain't trying to cause problems."

Ice didn't move. He knew men like Sonny all too well. They talked when things got tough, and they lied when their lives were on the line.

"You wanna play both sides?" Ice asked, his tone cold and measured. "You think you can flip and walk away clean?"

Sonny's face turned pale. He shook his head, sweat beading on his forehead. "I wasn't gonna say nothin'. I swear!"

Ice didn't hesitate. In one swift motion, he pulled the Glock from his waistband and pressed it to Sonny's forehead. Sonny's eyes went wide, his breath catching in his throat.

"Too late," Ice whispered.

The shot echoed through the small room, and Sonny

dropped to the floor, lifeless. Dre stood behind Ice, his face emotionless. This wasn't personal. It was business.

Ice lowered the gun, taking a step back. "Clean it up," he said to Dre, his voice cold. "No loose ends."

Dre nodded. "You got it."

As Ice walked out of the motel room, the weight of what he had just done didn't faze him. He had built his empire on control, power, and fear. And in this game, there was no room for weakness.

CHAPTER 10: CLOSING IN

The hit on Sonny sent shockwaves through Westbrook. Word traveled fast, and by morning, everyone knew what had happened. Rico's crew was left rattled, unsure of who was still loyal and who might be next. The streets were quieter than usual, as if they were holding their breath, waiting for the next move.

But Ice knew better than to get comfortable. Sonny's death was necessary to protect the empire, but it wouldn't stop the growing heat from the cops. If anything, it would put them on higher alert. He had snuffed out a rat, but the real challenge was staying ahead of the law.

Back at the penthouse, Dre filled Ice in on the aftermath.

"Rico's people are laying low," Dre said, leaning against the counter. "No one's making a move, but the cops? They're everywhere, asking questions."

Ice leaned back in his chair, his face unreadable. "They won't get anything."

Dre nodded, but his expression remained tense. "We took care of Sonny, but Rico's still out there. And now the cops are watching everything we do."

Ice knew Dre was right. Rico wasn't going to take Sonny's death lightly, and with the police circling, their options were limited. Ice needed to find a way to neutralize Rico without bringing more heat down on his crew.

"What's the word on Rico?" Ice asked.

"Last I heard, he's staying out of sight," Dre replied. "He's probably planning something, but no one knows what."

Ice's mind raced. He had built his empire on staying one step ahead, and now more than ever, he needed to maintain that edge. Rico was smart, but Ice had a plan.

"We're going to force his hand," Ice said, standing up. "He's on the ropes, but he won't stay there long. We need to make him come to us."

Dre frowned, confused. "How are we gonna do that?"

Ice's eyes gleamed with a cold determination. "We'll hit him where it hurts. His money. His people are scared, but they're loyal because he's paying them. We cut off the flow, and they'll turn on him."

That night, Ice and Dre took a small team and moved on one of Rico's biggest supply spots. It was a warehouse on the outskirts of the city—heavily guarded, but nothing Ice's crew couldn't handle.

They rolled up in three black SUVs, parking in the shadows, far enough from the warehouse to remain unnoticed. Ice had scouted the place for weeks, learning its weaknesses and how to exploit them. Tonight, they would hit hard and fast, taking out Rico's supply chain and forcing him into the open.

"We move quick," Ice said as his team gathered around him. "In and out. No mistakes."

The men nodded, gripping their weapons tightly. Ice could feel the tension in the air, the quiet before the storm.

Dre led the charge, creeping toward the warehouse with two of their best men. Ice followed close behind, his Glock in hand, every sense on high alert. They slipped through the side entrance, the silence broken only by the faint hum of machinery inside.

The warehouse was vast, dimly lit, and stacked with crates of product ready to be distributed across the city. Ice's eyes scanned the area, noting the guards posted at each corner. Rico had invested a lot in this place, but he hadn't counted on Ice knowing every inch of it.

Dre signaled the team, and within seconds, gunfire erupted. Ice moved swiftly, taking down one of the guards with a clean shot to the chest. The sound of bullets ricocheted through the warehouse as Dre's men pushed forward, hitting the guards with precision and speed.

Ice moved like a ghost through the chaos, his shots deliberate, calculated. The guards were unprepared, falling one by one as Ice's crew cleared the room. Within minutes, they had taken control of the entire warehouse, the air thick with the smell of gunpowder and blood.

Dre walked up to Ice, his shotgun still smoking. "We got it."

Ice nodded, his gaze turning to the crates stacked high against the walls. "Burn it."

Dre's eyes widened slightly. "Burn it all?"

Ice's expression was cold, unyielding. "All of it. Rico's about to feel this."

Without hesitation, Dre signaled the men. They moved quickly, dousing the crates with gasoline, setting the whole place up for destruction. Ice watched as the flames started to catch, licking up the sides of the warehouse, the heat intensifying with every second.

Within minutes, the warehouse was engulfed in fire, the flames consuming everything inside. Ice stood at the edge of the lot, watching as the flames danced in the night. Rico's supply chain was gone, and with it, his ability to control his crew.

"We just sent a message," Ice said, his voice low but powerful. "Now let's see how Rico responds."

As Ice and his team drove away, the glow of the fire fading in the distance, Ice knew the war with Rico had just taken a new turn. Rico would come for him, but Ice wasn't worried. He had forced Rico's hand, and now it was just a matter of time.

Back at the penthouse, Ice sat alone, staring out at the city lights. The streets of Westbrook were on edge, but Ice was ready for whatever came next. Rico's empire was crumbling, and soon, it would be Ice sitting at the top—undisputed.

CHAPTER 11: THE PRICE OF POWER

The fire at Rico's warehouse was all anyone in Westbrook could talk about. Ice's crew had hit Rico's operation hard, burning his supply and putting his empire on the ropes. The streets were buzzing with rumors of Rico's next move, but Ice wasn't worried. He had taken the first real shot, and now it was Rico's turn to respond.

But with every victory came a price.

Ice sat in his penthouse, his mind racing as he watched the news reports of the warehouse fire. The media painted it as an accident, but everyone in the streets knew what had really happened. Rico's men were scrambling, and without his supply, his power was slipping.

Dre walked into the room, looking grim. "You sure about this, Ice? Rico's not the type to just let something like this slide."

Ice's gaze stayed on the TV screen. "He'll come for us. I know that. But he's playing from behind now. We've got the advantage."

Dre sighed, sitting down across from Ice. "Yeah, but the heat's getting stronger. The cops are watching every move we make. We hit him again, and we could bring too much attention to ourselves."

Ice knew Dre was right. The police had been circling ever since the shootout, and now with the fire, things were getting more intense. But Ice couldn't afford to slow down. He was too close to the top to stop now.

"We stay low for a bit," Ice said, his voice calm but firm. "Let Rico make the next move. We'll be ready."

Dre nodded, but the tension between them lingered. They both knew the risks, and as much as Ice had planned for this moment, the weight of it was starting to take its toll.

Later that night, Ice sat on the edge of his bed, his hands resting on his knees. Tasha lay beside him, her eyes watching him closely. She had seen the change in him over the past few weeks—the pressure, the constant threat of violence, the endless cycle of power and control.

"You don't have to do this, you know," she said softly, reaching out to touch his arm. "You've got enough money. You could walk away from all of this."

Ice didn't respond right away. He stared at the floor, his mind torn between the life he had built and the cost of keeping it. Walking away wasn't an option—not now. Not when he was so close to having everything.

"This is all I know," Ice finally said, his voice low. "I've come too far to walk away now."

Tasha sighed, sitting up beside him. "I just don't want to lose you. Every time you leave, I wonder if it's the last time I'll see you."

Ice turned to her, his expression softening. He reached out, brushing a strand of hair from her face. “You won’t lose me.”

But even as he said the words, he could feel the weight of uncertainty pressing down on him. The streets were a battlefield, and no matter how good you were, no one was untouchable.

The next day, Dre showed up at Ice’s penthouse, his face tense with urgency. Ice could tell by the look in his eyes that something was wrong.

“We got a problem,” Dre said, closing the door behind him.

Ice’s body tensed. “What is it?”

“Rico’s men—they hit one of our spots last night. Burned it down just like we did to them,” Dre said, his voice tight with frustration. “They’re sending a message.”

Ice stood up, his jaw clenched. “How bad?”

“Bad,” Dre replied. “We lost a shipment. Rico’s crew was in and out before we even knew what was happening.”

Ice paced the room, his mind racing. He had expected Rico to strike back, but the hit on their shipment was a major blow. Rico wasn’t going to back down, and the war between them was escalating faster than Ice had anticipated.

“They want a war, they’ll get one,” Ice muttered under his breath.

Dre looked at him, concern etched on his face. “You sure about this, Ice? The cops are watching. Another hit, and we’ll be neck-deep in heat.”

Ice didn't hesitate. "We're not letting Rico take what's ours. We hit him harder. But we do it smart. No more noise."

Dre nodded, but the tension between them lingered. The stakes were higher than ever, and both men knew that one wrong move could cost them everything.

That night, Ice called a meeting with his top lieutenants. The penthouse was quiet, the weight of what they were about to discuss hanging heavy in the air.

"We're going to shut Rico down for good," Ice said, his voice cold and sharp. "But we're not doing it out in the open. We go after his money. His people are already scared. We take away his cash flow, and he'll have no one left to fight for him."

The men nodded, their eyes locked on Ice. They trusted him, but they knew the risks. Rico was dangerous, and taking him down wouldn't be easy.

"We hit his stash houses," Ice continued. "One by one. No noise, no bodies. Just his money. We drain him dry, and then we finish it."

Dre glanced at the men around the room before speaking. "We hit those spots quietly, we could take Rico out without the cops breathing down our necks."

Ice nodded. "That's the plan. We do this right, and Rico's done."

CHAPTER 12: THE SILENT STRIKE

Ice's plan was in motion, and the next move was crucial. The war with Rico had escalated, and now it was a battle of strategy, not just firepower. The plan to drain Rico's resources was bold, but if executed right, it would leave him without the money or manpower to fight back.

The night was thick with tension as Ice, Dre, and a small crew of trusted men pulled up near one of Rico's stash houses. It was located in a quiet, unassuming neighborhood—far from the chaos of the streets, but Ice knew better. Rico had hidden a lot of his operations in plain sight, and tonight, Ice was about to cut off a major artery of Rico's empire.

Ice and his crew moved like shadows, their movements silent as they approached the house. The plan was simple: get in, grab the cash, and leave without making any noise. The fewer people that knew they had been there, the better.

Dre signaled the team, and they moved in. The house was guarded, but Ice's crew was well-prepared. The guards were caught off guard—silenced before they even had a chance to react. Ice watched from the shadows, his Glock ready, but his focus was on the mission. Tonight wasn't about killing.

It was about taking control.

Inside the house, they found what they had been looking for. Stacks of cash, neatly packed in duffel bags, ready to be moved. Rico had been using this spot to funnel money through the city, but now, that flow was about to dry up.

"Bag it all," Ice ordered, his voice low but commanding.

Dre and the others worked quickly, stuffing the cash into their own bags. They moved with precision, knowing that every second counted. The more they took, the harder it would be for Rico to keep his people loyal.

As they packed up the last of the money, Dre turned to Ice, a smirk on his face. "We're gonna bleed this dude dry."

Ice nodded, his expression cold. "This is just the start."

With the bags full, Ice and his crew slipped out of the house, leaving no trace behind. The operation had been flawless, and as they drove away, Ice felt the weight of the night's success settle over him. Rico was losing control, and soon, he'd have nothing left.

Back at the penthouse, Ice and Dre unloaded the duffel bags, the cash spilling out onto the table. It was a small fortune, but to Ice, it was more than just money. It was a message.

Dre leaned back, lighting a blunt as he stared at the piles of cash. "This is it, man. Rico's gotta be feeling this by now."

Ice nodded, his mind already planning the next move. "We hit another spot tomorrow. Keep the pressure on. He'll crumble."

Dre exhaled, the smoke curling in the air. "And when he

does?"

Ice's eyes narrowed. "We take everything."

The next few days were a blur of action. Ice's crew hit stash house after stash house, each time draining more of Rico's resources. The hits were quick, quiet, and ruthless. Rico's men were caught off guard, and with every loss, his grip on the streets loosened. Word spread fast that Rico was losing control, and as his money dried up, so did the loyalty of his crew.

The streets of Westbrook were changing, and Ice could feel the power shifting in his favor.

But with every move, the tension grew. Rico was backed into a corner, and Ice knew that a man with nothing left to lose was the most dangerous kind.

One night, as Ice sat in his penthouse, going over the latest reports from Dre, his phone buzzed. It was an unknown number, but Ice had a feeling he knew who it was.

He answered, his voice steady. "This Ice."

There was a pause on the other end, and then a familiar voice came through, low and filled with venom. "You think you've won, huh?"

It was Rico.

Ice didn't flinch. "I'm not thinking. I know."

Rico laughed bitterly. "You've been hitting my spots, taking my money. But you know what they say, Ice—when you back a wolf into a corner, he bites."

Ice leaned back in his chair, calm but focused. "I'm not

worried about your bite, Rico. I'm taking what's mine. And soon, you'll have nothing left."

Rico's tone grew darker. "You're making a mistake. You think you can just take everything from me and walk away? You think I'm gonna let that happen?"

Ice's grip tightened on the phone, his voice cold as ice. "I already have."

Rico's laugh was harsh, filled with fury. "This ain't over. Not by a long shot. You took my money, but you can't take me down. You're coming for the king, and you better not miss."

Before Ice could respond, the line went dead. He stared at the phone, his mind racing. Rico was desperate, but desperation made people reckless. Ice knew that Rico was planning something big, and whatever it was, it would be his last stand.

Later that night, Ice called Dre and his top lieutenants into the penthouse. The atmosphere was tense, the weight of the war with Rico pressing down on everyone.

"Rico's coming for us," Ice said, his voice calm but filled with authority. "He's got nothing left but pride, and that makes him dangerous."

Dre nodded, his expression serious. "What's the move?"

Ice's eyes glinted with cold determination. "We hit him first. We take him out before he has the chance to make a move."

The room fell silent. Everyone knew what this meant. They had taken Rico's money, his power, but now it was time to finish the job. It was time to end the war, once and for all.

CHAPTER 13: THE LAST STAND

The city of Westbrook was like a pressure cooker ready to explode. The air felt thick, charged with tension, as the streets buzzed with rumors about the final clash between Ice and Rico. Everyone knew it was coming. Ice had taken everything from Rico—his money, his crew, and now all that remained was to take his life. Ice was ready for whatever came next, but he knew this wasn't going to be easy. Rico had nothing left to lose, and desperate men didn't follow the rules.

Ice sat in his penthouse, surrounded by Dre and his top lieutenants. The plan to finish Rico was already in motion. They had pinpointed Rico's last stronghold, a rundown hideout on the far side of the city, where he was holed up with the few loyal men he had left.

"We end this tonight," Ice said, his voice steady and cold. "No more games. We take him out, and we take the streets."

Dre nodded, his face serious. "You think Rico knows we're coming?"

Ice leaned back, his fingers tapping lightly on the table. "He knows. But he's cornered. He'll try to hit us hard, but we've got the upper hand. We go in smart, no mistakes."

The men around the table exchanged looks, each one knowing that tonight would be the end of the war, one way or another.

As the night settled in, Ice and his crew rolled out in three black SUVs, heading toward Rico's hideout. The city lights blurred past as they drove through the streets, silent and focused. There was no room for error tonight. They were going to take Rico out, once and for all.

Ice sat in the lead SUV, his Glock resting on his lap, his mind racing through every possible scenario. He had been waiting for this moment, preparing for it, but he knew the unpredictability of the streets. Rico wouldn't go down easily, and Ice needed to be ready for anything.

When they arrived at Rico's hideout, the area was eerily quiet. The building was dark, no sign of life inside. But Ice knew better. Rico was waiting for them, and the real battle was about to begin.

Dre and the rest of the crew moved in, guns drawn, moving silently toward the building. Ice followed, his senses heightened, every sound around him amplified. They approached the front entrance, the tension building with every step.

Without a word, Ice nodded to Dre, who kicked the door in. The crew moved fast, sweeping through the first floor, guns ready. The place was run-down, abandoned-looking, but Ice knew Rico was there. He could feel it.

Suddenly, gunfire erupted from the second floor. The air filled with the deafening sound of bullets as Rico's men opened fire. Ice and his crew ducked behind cover, returning fire with precision. The battle had begun.

"Upstairs!" Ice shouted, signaling his men to move.

Dre led the charge up the stairs, blasting away at anything that moved. Ice followed close behind, his Glock raised, firing off shots at Rico's men. The hallway was a war zone—bullets ricocheting off walls, bodies dropping left and right. The air was thick with smoke and the smell of gunpowder.

Ice moved like a machine, his aim deadly, his focus unbreakable. He could see the desperation in Rico's crew as they fought, but they were no match for Ice's calculated precision. One by one, they fell, until only a few remained.

As they cleared the second floor, Ice knew Rico was close. He pushed forward, his heart pounding, his senses sharp. This was it—the final moment.

Ice kicked open the door to the last room, his gun raised, ready to fire. Inside, Rico stood alone, a gun in his hand, his face twisted with rage and desperation.

"Ice," Rico spat, his voice filled with venom. "You really think you can take everything from me and just walk away?"

Ice stepped into the room, his Glock aimed directly at Rico's chest. "I already did. This is over."

Rico laughed bitterly, his eyes wild. "You don't know what you've done. You think this ends with me? You're just a pawn in a game you don't even understand."

Ice's expression didn't change. He had heard it all before—men who couldn't accept they had lost, trying to convince themselves they were still in control.

"This is my game now," Ice said coldly. "And you're done."

Rico raised his gun, but he wasn't fast enough. Ice fired first. The shot rang out, echoing through the room as Rico staggered back, blood spilling from his chest. He collapsed to the floor, his gun slipping from his hand.

Ice stepped closer, standing over Rico as he lay dying. Rico's eyes locked onto Ice's, filled with anger and disbelief. He had been the king of these streets for so long, but now, he was nothing.

"You... don't... win," Rico choked out, blood bubbling from his mouth.

Ice stared down at him, his expression cold. "I already did."

With that, Rico took his last breath. The war was over.

The room was silent now, the only sound the faint creak of the building settling. Ice lowered his gun, taking a deep breath. The streets had belonged to Rico for years, but now they were Ice's. He had fought for this, bled for this, and now he had won.

Dre stepped into the room, glancing down at Rico's body. "It's done."

Ice nodded, his mind already moving to the next steps. "We clean this up. No traces. Rico's gone, and now we run the streets."

Dre grinned, nodding. "We made it, Ice."

But Ice wasn't smiling. He had won the war, but the cost of power was heavy. He knew the battles weren't over—there would always be someone trying to take what he had built. But for now, Westbrook belonged to him.

CHAPTER 14: AFTER THE THRONE

The war was over, but the streets of Westbrook were still buzzing with the aftermath. Rico was gone, his empire dismantled, and Ice stood alone as the undisputed king of the city. But the victory, while sweet, brought with it a new kind of pressure. The throne came with a heavy price, and everyone in the game knew that someone else would soon try to take what Ice had earned.

Back at the penthouse, the mood was celebratory. Dre, Tasha, and the rest of the crew sat around, toasting to the victory. The war had been long and brutal, but they had won. Ice's name now carried more weight than ever, and the city was theirs.

"We did it," Dre said, raising his glass. "Rico's gone, and now we run this place."

The crew cheered, raising their drinks to Ice, but Ice himself sat quietly, his thoughts far away from the celebration. He stared out of the window, watching the city lights flicker below. The victory had come at a cost, and Ice felt the weight of everything he had done to get here.

Tasha walked over, her eyes scanning his face. "You alright?"

Ice didn't respond right away. He let out a long breath, his mind racing with everything that had happened. He had taken down Rico, he had won the war, but what came next? The streets were always hungry for the next power, the next king, and Ice knew that his time at the top wouldn't last forever.

"I'm good," Ice finally said, his voice low.

Tasha sat beside him, resting her hand on his. "You've been quiet since... since it all went down."

Ice nodded, staring out at the skyline. "It's just... this ain't what I thought it'd feel like."

Tasha's gaze softened. "You've done what you had to do, Jay. You built this empire. It's yours."

Ice turned to her, his eyes heavy with the weight of the streets. "Yeah. But I had to bury a lot of people to get here."

Tasha understood. She had seen him go through it all—the rise, the violence, the bloodshed. She knew that the crown he wore was built on pain and sacrifice.

The days after Rico's death were a blur of business and restructuring. Ice took full control of the city, making moves to secure every corner, every deal. Rico's old men either fell in line or disappeared. The streets had shifted, and everyone knew that Ice was the new power.

But the police were still watching. The war with Rico had left a trail, and the cops were circling, waiting for Ice to slip up. The tension was palpable, and Ice knew he couldn't afford to make any mistakes.

One afternoon, Dre came to Ice with troubling news. "The

Feds are sniffing around, man. They're asking questions about Rico's disappearance. They're looking for someone to pin it on."

Ice's jaw tightened. He had been careful, but no one could stay invisible forever. The streets might have accepted him as king, but the law was a different beast entirely.

"We keep everything clean," Ice said. "No slips. No heat. They won't find anything."

But Dre looked uneasy. "They're getting close, Ice. Too close. We gotta start thinking about an exit plan."

Ice's mind churned. He had worked too hard to build his empire, and the idea of walking away didn't sit right with him. But Dre was right. The Feds were closing in, and staying in the game too long was a risk.

"We're not running," Ice finally said, his voice steady. "But we'll tighten things up. Keep the heat off us."

Later that night, Ice sat alone in his office, the weight of the game pressing down on him harder than ever. The streets had been his life for so long, but the longer he stayed, the more dangerous it became. He had outplayed Rico, but the law wasn't something you could outgun or outmaneuver forever.

As Ice stared at the stacks of cash on his desk, the phone rang. It was Tasha.

"You coming home tonight?" she asked, her voice soft.

Ice glanced at the clock. It was late, and he hadn't even realized how much time had passed.

"Yeah, I'll be there soon," Ice replied, his voice distant.

But as he hung up the phone, a sense of unease settled over him. The life he had built, the power he had claimed—it had come at a cost. And now, Ice was starting to wonder if the price had been too high.

The next morning, Dre showed up at the penthouse, his face serious.

"We need to talk," Dre said, closing the door behind him.

Ice leaned back in his chair, sensing the tension in Dre's voice. "What's up?"

Dre took a deep breath. "I've been hearing things. People talking about taking you down. Not just the Feds—other crews. They're seeing an opening."

Ice's eyes narrowed. "Who's talking?"

Dre hesitated for a moment. "A lot of small crews. They think they can make a move now that Rico's gone. They don't know what they're up against."

Ice's jaw clenched. He had just finished one war, and now another one was already brewing. The streets didn't sleep, and no matter how high you climbed, someone was always waiting to take your spot.

"We shut it down," Ice said, his voice cold. "Anyone talking about making a move, we make sure they know who's in charge."

Dre nodded, but there was a flicker of doubt in his eyes. "Ice… you know how this goes. The higher you climb, the harder the fall."

Ice didn't respond. He knew Dre was right, but walking away wasn't an option. Not now. He had worked too hard to build this empire, and he wasn't about to let anyone take it from him.

CHAPTER 15: THE INEVITABLE END

The city streets of Westbrook had changed under Ice's rule, but not in the way he had imagined. With Rico gone and his empire firmly in Ice's grasp, there was an eerie calm that settled over the city. But it was the kind of calm that comes just before a storm, and Ice knew it. The whispers were growing louder—the Feds were closing in, and rival crews were plotting in the shadows.

Ice stood in his penthouse, looking out at the skyline that he once saw as a symbol of his rise. Now, it felt more like a prison. The weight of the streets had become heavier than ever, and no matter how much money or power he accumulated, there was always another threat, another fire to put out.

Dre entered the room, his expression serious, the tension palpable between them.

"We got some real trouble now, Ice," Dre said. "It's not just the small crews anymore. Word is, bigger names are getting involved—outside hitters. They're coming for you."

Ice didn't flinch, though his mind was already racing. Outside hitters meant that the street-level war was escalating beyond Westbrook. Rival gangs from neighboring cities had heard of Rico's downfall and saw it as an opportunity to take over the lucrative drug market Ice controlled.

"We still hold all the cards," Ice said, his voice cold. "They won't take us out that easily."

Dre sighed, running a hand over his face. "It's not just the streets, man. The Feds are closing in hard. They've got wiretaps, surveillance—they're building a case. I don't know how much longer we can stay ahead of this."

Ice leaned against the windowsill, his jaw tight. He had always known that the Feds would come, but he hadn't expected it to happen this fast, especially after dealing with Rico. Now, with the added pressure of rival gangs and the law closing in, the walls were starting to close around him.

"What do you think?" Ice asked, his voice quieter than usual.

Dre hesitated, his loyalty clear, but there was fear in his eyes. "We've been in this game a long time, Ice. And we've won a lot of battles, but there's no winning against the Feds. They're patient, and they never stop."

Ice nodded slowly, the truth of Dre's words sinking in. It wasn't just about power anymore. He had all the money, all the control—but in the end, the game had always been rigged. The streets had their rules, but the law didn't play by those rules.

That night, Ice sat alone in the darkened living room, the weight of everything pressing down on him. He had built an empire, fought off rivals, and taken down Rico. He had everything he thought he wanted—but now, he realized that he was trapped in a world that would never let him go.

The sound of footsteps broke the silence, and Tasha appeared in the doorway. She had been watching him closely for weeks, seeing the toll the streets had taken on him.

"You don't have to do this, Jay," she said softly, sitting beside him. "You can walk away. We can walk away."

Ice let out a deep breath. He had heard it before, but this time it felt different. The money, the power—it had all come at a cost he wasn't sure he could pay anymore.

"Walking away isn't that simple," Ice replied, his voice hollow.

Tasha reached for his hand, her grip firm but gentle. "It can be. You've done enough, Jay. You've made your mark. You don't have to keep fighting."

Ice closed his eyes, the temptation of her words tugging at him. He had always seen himself as unstoppable, but now he could feel the cracks forming. The streets didn't offer a way out—not without consequences.

"I don't know if I can," Ice whispered, the vulnerability in his voice foreign to him.

Tasha leaned closer, her voice barely above a whisper. "You can. You just have to decide."

The next morning, Ice called a meeting with Dre and the top lieutenants. They gathered in the penthouse, the tension thick in the air. Everyone knew that things were reaching a breaking point.

"We're being squeezed from both sides," Ice said, pacing the room. "The streets are moving against us, and the Feds are closing in. We need to make a move—now."

Dre crossed his arms, his face grim. "What are you thinking?"

Ice stopped pacing, turning to face his crew. "We take what we can and get out. We've got enough money stashed away to disappear. If we stay, it's only a matter of time before the Feds or one of these crews takes us down."

The room was silent. The men exchanged glances, some nodding in agreement, others unsure. They had fought for years to build this empire, and now Ice was asking them to walk away.

"We've been at the top," Ice continued, his voice steady but filled with urgency. "But staying in the game too long is how you lose everything. We cash out, and we leave this life behind."

Dre sighed heavily but nodded. "You know I'm with you, Ice. Whatever you decide."

One by one, the lieutenants agreed. The writing was on the wall—staying in Westbrook would only lead to a downfall, whether by the hands of rival crews or the Feds.

The decision was made. Ice and his crew would disappear, leaving behind the streets they had once ruled. Over the next few days, they moved quickly, pulling money from their hidden stashes, securing fake identities, and planning their escape. It was a risky move, but it was the only way out.

As the plan unfolded, Ice felt a strange sense of peace. He had built an empire from nothing, and now he was walking away from it all. But he knew it was the only way to survive.

On the night of their planned departure, Ice stood on the balcony of his penthouse, looking out over the city one last time. Westbrook had been his battlefield, his kingdom, but now it was time to let it go.

Tasha joined him on the balcony, her hand slipping into his. "You ready?"

Ice didn't answer right away. He took a deep breath, his gaze lingering on the city lights below. For the first time in a long time, he felt the weight lifting from his shoulders.

"Yeah," he finally said. "I'm ready."

With that, Ice turned away from the city he had once ruled, ready to start a new life far from the streets that had defined him for so long. The king of ice was stepping down, but for the first time, he felt free.

Made in the USA
Middletown, DE
15 October 2024